W9-AXD-062

LOLA  FRED

Heuer

# Lola &Fred

4N Publishing

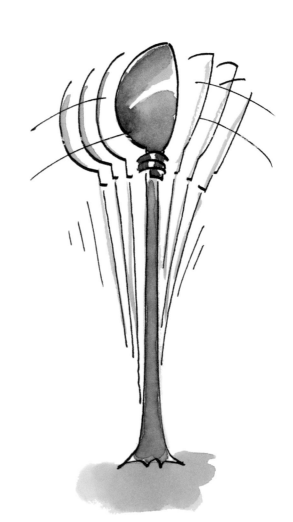

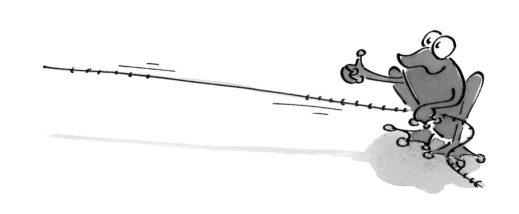

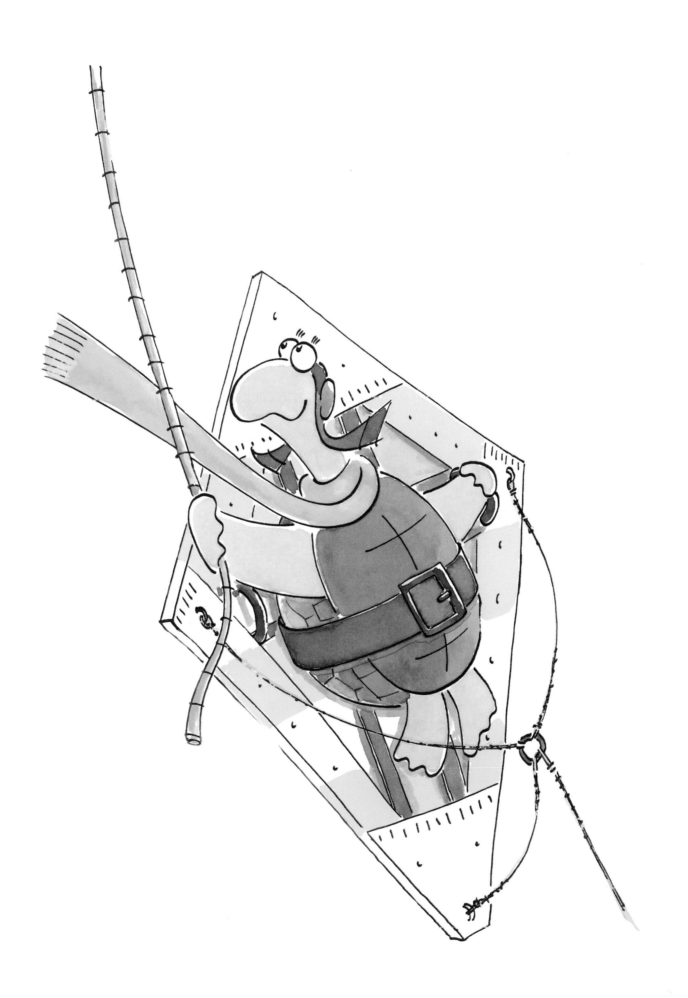

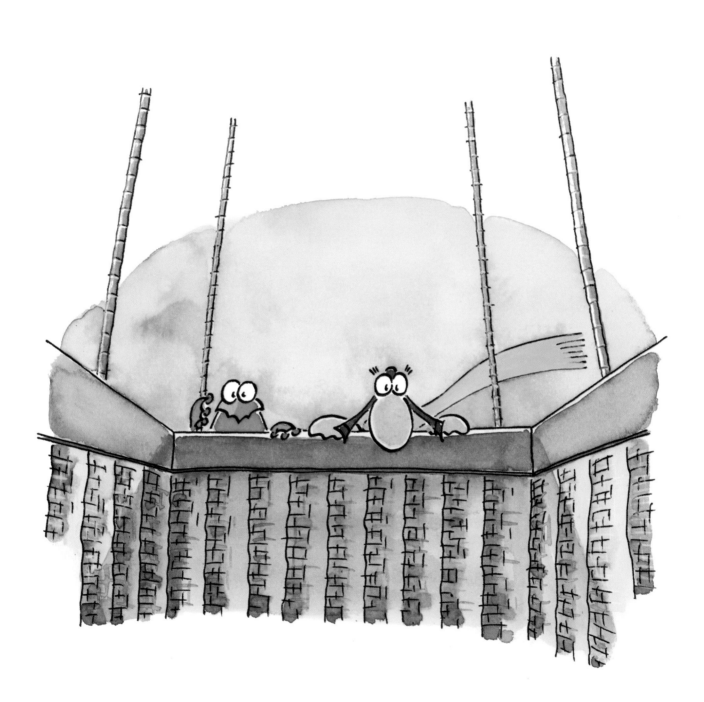

"Lola & Fred"
ISBN : 0-9741319-8-9

Printed in Singapore by Tien Wah Press

Visit www.4npublishing.com to receive information on other 4N books.
Visit www.pul.ch to receive more information on Christoph Heuer.